MATT CHRISTOPHER
SPORTS READERS!

THE DOG THAT STOLE FOOTBALL PLAYS

978-1-59953-350-6

THE DOG THAT CALLED THE SIGNALS

978-1-59953-349-0

THE DOG THAT PITCHED A NO-HITTER

978-1-59953-351-3

THE DOG THAT STOLE HOME

978-1-59953-352-0

THE DOG THAT CALLED THE PITCH

978-1-59953-353-7

READ ALL THE BOOKS IN THE SERIES!

MATT CHRISTOPHER
SPORTS READERS

THE DOG THAT CALLED THE SIGNALS

Illustrated by Bill Ogden

NORWOOD HOUSE PRESS

CHICAGO, ILLINOIS

To Melanie

Norwood House Press
P.O. Box 316598
Chicago, Illinois 60631

For information regarding Norwood House Press, please visit our website at: www.norwoodhousepress.com or call 866-565-2900.

This library edition was published in 2010.

Library of Congress Cataloging-in-Publication Data:
Christopher, Matt.
  The dog that called the signals / Matt Christopher.
    p. cm. — (Matt Christopher sports readers)
  Summary: During a crucial football game, Mike, the quarterback, gets help from his unusual dog Harry when his coach gets hurt and cannot call the plays from home.
  ISBN-13: 978-1-59953-349-0 (lib. ed. : alk. paper)
  ISBN-10: 1-59953-349-9 (lib. ed. : alk. paper)
  (1. Dogs—Fiction. 2. Football—Fiction. 3. Telepathy—Fiction. 4. Teamwork (Sports)—Fiction.) I. Title.
  PZ7.C458Dn 2010
  (E)—dc22
                          2009043059

Manufactured in the United States of America in North Mankato, Minnesota.
N146—012010

Mike and his dog, Harry the Airedale, had walked from the field across the empty lot to Coach Hawkins's house. They were now seated in the living room trying to give the coach a message.

"Bad news, Coach," Mike began. "We won't have —"

"Pass it to Barker, Tip! To Barker!" Coach Hawkins shouted, interrupting Mike.

The coach was sitting on the edge of his chair in front of a television set, watching a football game and waving his arms excitedly.

"Attaboy! Now run with it, Barker! Run! Good boy! Five yards! Ten! Good run, Barker!"

Mike glanced down at his dog and shrugged. "We came at the wrong time, Harry," he said, disappointed.

"Yeah," Harry agreed. "But keep butting in. He's sure to hear you after a while."

"I hope so," thought Mike.

As far as Mike knew, Harry was the most unusual dog in the world. Mike had found Harry in a pet shop and had discovered that the dog could communi-

cate with him by mental telepathy. He
had brought Harry home that day and
they had been friends ever since.

Mike looked from Harry to the coach.
"I bet he's forgotten why he asked us
in," Mike thought.

Suddenly the big man glanced around at them, and an apologetic smile came over his round face. "Sorry, Mike," he said. "But I just had to watch that play. What can I do for you?"

"I just saw Bobby Doan," Mike explained. "He can't quarterback the team in next Saturday's game. He and his family are going on a vacation."

"He *what?*" The coach rolled his eyes up toward the ceiling and slapped his knees, frustrated. "Of all the lousy luck! Well, there's only one thing to do, Mike. *You* will have to play quarterback."

"Me?"

"Yes, you. I know you don't have much experience, but you've tried hard in practice. There's a lot at stake in that game, kid," the coach said seriously. "The Number Seven Firemen, our team's sponsor, promised us new uniforms if we beat the Browns. And you know how badly we need uniforms. Ours are beginning to look like rags."

"Yeah," Mike agreed.

"I think you can do it, kid," said the coach. "Just go home and study your playbook. And now that that's settled, please excuse me."

He turned his attention back to the football game on the TV set, watched it a few seconds, and began yelling again: "Run it through right tackle, Jim! Right tackle! Attaboy! See that?" he said to Mike. "He played it just as if he had heard me!"

"Right. Well, see you at practice, Coach," Mike said quietly. He walked out of the house, Harry trotting at his side.

"He sure gets wrapped up in football games, doesn't he?" remarked Harry.

"He sure does," said Mike. "But he

lives by himself and he must not have much company. I guess that's why he likes getting out and coaching us."

"I suppose," replied Harry, "but he lives almost close enough to the field to coach us from his back porch."

They reached the intersection, waited for the light to change, then crossed the street.

"Harry, I can't play quarterback," Mike said, thinking of all the things a quarterback had to do. "I'm a better linebacker. I don't know a thing about calling signals."

"Well, as you humans say, it's never too late to learn," said Harry.

"Yeah, sure," Mike shot back, and they glumly walked home.

The Jets practiced on Tuesday, and Coach Hawkins had Mike work out at the quarterback slot.

He didn't do very well. Twice he fumbled the ball, and three times he threw passes that were either too far beyond, or too far short of, the receivers. He felt terrible.

"Coach, I'm playing lousy," he complained. "Can't you get someone else to play quarterback?"

The coach patted him on the shoulder. "Settle down, Mike," he said encouragingly. "You'll do okay."

"Sure, he will. Except for two passes that sailed over my head he was great," Butch Stevens, the right side wide receiver, snickered.

In Thursday's practice Mike figured he played worse than he had on Tuesday. His long passes to Butch, and to Tom Reed, the wide receiver on the left side, were way off and he had trouble remembering which plays to call.

"Concentrate and try throwing shorter passes, Mike," the coach suggested.

Mike did, and discovered that he could throw them on target better than he could the longer ones. He felt a little better.

"Nice going." Harry's pleased words came into his thoughts from the sideline. Harry, Mike saw, was standing next to the coach.

A little later Mike glanced over and saw Coach Hawkins scratching Harry's head. Harry seemed to enjoy it, judging from the silly look on his face.

"I guess the coach has gotten to like the little monkey," Mike thought, smiling to himself.

"Dog, Mike, not monkey," Harry's thoughts shot back to him. "I sure hope you know the difference."

Mike's face turned red. "I sure do, and I'm sorry, Harry," he apologized.

The team practiced again on Friday, hoping to be well prepared for Saturday's game against the Browns. They had to win it, or their chance to get brand-new uniforms would go down the drain.

Mike was amused by the friendship that had developed between his dog and the coach. "I just hope that they don't start reading each other's mind like we do," he told himself. "I like Harry being special to me."

"Relax, pal," Harry's thoughts came through to him. "I have tried to talk with him. It didn't work. Satisfied?"

Mike grinned. "Satisfied!"

Harry was just a dog, but that brain of his was working every minute.

Saturday came, and Mike walked to
the game with Harry at his side. In spite
of the coach's telling him not to worry,
Mike still felt butterflies in his stomach.
Why did Bobby Doan have to go on a
vacation this weekend, anyway?

They reached the football field, and Mike compared his Jets' worn, tattered uniform with the Browns' spanking new ones. "What a mess," he thought.

"In more ways than one," Harry said.

Just before the game started Harry ran over to Coach Hawkins's side and trotted back and forth with him behind the sideline. Mike laughed at the sight, and so did a lot of other people.

The Jets won the toss, and Mike chose to receive. The Browns kicked off. Butch caught the ball and ran it back to the Jets' twenty-six-yard line. But, in the huddle, Mike panicked and wasn't sure what play to call.

"Quit stalling or we'll get penalized," Butch said.

"Eighteen pass," Mike said quickly.

The guys stared at him. "What? A pass play the first thing?" Larry Curtis said.

Mike looked nervously at him.

The team lined up, and Mike called signals. Sweat poured off his face. Larry was right. Calling for a pass on the first play was stupid.

He got the ball from center, and half a dozen Browns broke through the line and swarmed on him before he could throw it. An eight-yard loss!

Mike called for an end-around run on the next play and lost two more yards. Third and twenty to go. What a lousy start!

More sweat poured down his face.

What play should he call now? He thought again of the eighteen pass play, and called it.

This time he fumbled the ball, but fell on it in time.

Frank Tooney, the fullback, punted it to get it as far away from the Jets' end zone as possible. But in two plays the Browns ran it back down to the Jets' eight-yard line. Then they tried a pass.

Mike, playing safety, intercepted it in the end zone! He dodged several Browns players, stiff-armed two, tripped over another's legs, got his balance, then ran all the rest of the way for a touchdown!

"What great open field running!" Butch cried, slapping him on the back.

Mike, breathing hard, couldn't believe
it. He had scored a touchdown!
"Nice run, pal," said Harry.
"Thanks, Harry!" said Mike.

After the kickoff the Jets got lucky again; the Browns fumbled the ball, and Frank pounced on it.

From the huddle Mike looked behind him, and shook. They were ten yards from the Browns' goal line!

He turned and looked at the ten faces waiting for him to call a play. But what play should he call? What play could get them nearer to that goal line?

"Let me run it," Frank piped up.

"Throw me a pass," said Larry.

"Fake a pass, then hand it off to me," Butch suggested.

Suddenly all the other players tried to tell Mike what play to call. He was so confused he didn't know what to do.

A whistle shrilled. "Delay of game!"

shouted the ref. "Five yards penalty!"

Now the ball was *fifteen* yards from the Browns' goal line!

Suddenly a substitute came running in from the Jets' bench. "The coach says try a short pass to Larry," he said to Mike, then told one of the other players to leave.

Mike tried the pass. And it worked. They scored!

Again and again in the first quarter the coach sent in plays from the bench. Sometimes they didn't work, but most of the time they did.

Mike felt relieved. As long as the coach kept sending in the plays, the Jets had a good chance of winning the game. And earning their new uniforms, too.

Then, in the middle of the second quarter, something happened. Coach Hawkins, who had been pacing back and forth at the sideline, let out a yell and suddenly fell down.

Both teams stopped moving and stared at him lying on the grass.

"He's hurt!" Mike cried, and sprinted toward the sideline. The others took off after him.

"What happened, Coach?" Mike asked
when he reached him.

"Sprained my ankle in that doggone
hole!" Coach Hawkins said, pointing at a
small hole in the ground behind him.

"Oh, no!" Mike wailed. Harry, crouched next to the coach, looked up.

"Don't look at me just because he said 'doggone,' " said Harry. "It wasn't my fault."

"Who said it was?" Mike replied. He looked back at the coach. "What do you want us to do, Coach?"

"Win this ball game," answered the coach. "But you'll have to do it without me. I'm going home to take care of this ankle. This time you've *got* to run the team."

Mike's face dropped.

"Mind if I take your pooch with me?" the coach went on. "I can watch the game through my field glasses and enjoy his company at the same time. How about it?"

Mike and Harry exchanged glances. "Is it okay with you?" Mike asked.

"Sure, if it's okay with you," said Harry. "After all, I am your dog."

Mike agreed to let Harry go with the coach. A friend of Coach Hawkins's then helped him off the field, and Harry left with them.

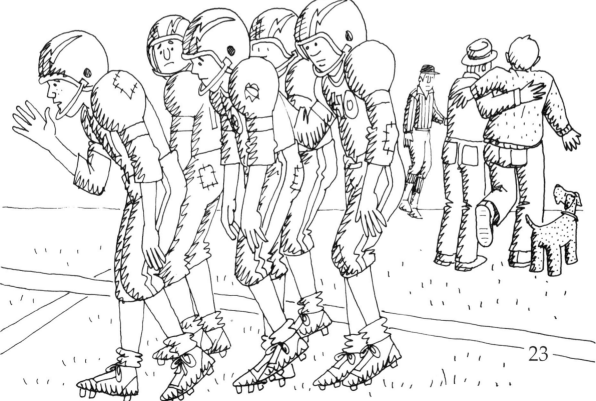

Mike shook his head sadly as he turned his attention back to his team- mates. "Guys, we can kiss those uni- forms good-bye," he said, and headed back onto the field. "Come on. Let's fin- ish the game."

Within five minutes the Browns scored two touchdowns on a run through right tackle, and made both kicks for the extra point good. Jets 14, Browns 14.

In the third quarter the Browns scored two more times, but they missed the kick for the extra point once. Jets 14, Browns 27.

As his team started to lose, Mike got more and more mixed up about which play to call. He had never wished so badly for a game to end. Of all the times for the coach to sprain an ankle.

Suddenly a voice cut into his unhappy thoughts. "Mike! Hey, Mike! Are you listening?"

"Don't bother me, Harry," he said. "It's our ball and I've got to figure out something —"

"I know!" Harry's excited thoughts came through to him as clear as a bell.

"The coach got his ankle taped and now he's watching the game from his porch through his field glasses. And he's yelling 'razzle-dazzle!' "

"Razzle-dazzle? Hey, that's great! The razzle-dazzle, guys!" Mike ordered. "Let's go!"

The play had the Browns running back and forth on the field like crazy, wondering which Jet had the ball.

Butch finished the run by scoring a touchdown. Then Frank kicked the extra point. Browns 27, Jets 21.

"It worked! It worked!" Mike shouted.

The game went into the fourth quarter. Every time the Jets had the ball Mike called a signal that Harry gave to him from the coach. And almost every time the team tried it, it worked for at least a few yards.

Then, with only a minute left to play, Mike tried the razzle-dazzle again. This time Tom got the ball and sprinted down the field for another touchdown! And Frank kicked the ball between the up-rights for the extra point!

Seconds later the game was over. Jets 28, Browns 27.

"Number Seven Firemen — bring on those new uniforms!" the guys cried happily.

Butch slapped Mike enthusiastically on the back. "Thanks to Mike, our great quarterback!" he said.

Mike smiled, and wished he could tell the guys who was really responsible for their win. But he had promised Harry he would never reveal their secret to anyone.

As the Jets headed for the locker room Mike saw his dog come bounding across the field toward him.

"Harry!" he cried as Harry leaped up into his arms. "You've got more brains than a barrel of monkeys!"

"Doggone right!" Harry replied, and licked Mike's cheeks.